Gallery Books
Editor: Peter Fallon

THE RAINMAKERS

Francis Harvey

THE RAINMAKERS

Gallery Books

The Rainmakers
is first published
simultaneously in paperback
and in a clothbound edition
in August 1988.

The Gallery Press
19 Oakdown Road
Dublin 14, Ireland

All rights reserved

© Francis Harvey 1978, 1988

ISBN 1 85235 024 5 (*paperback*)
     1 85235 025 3 (*clothbound*)

Acknowledgements
Acknowledgement is made to the editors of *Cyphers*, *The Donegal Democrat* (The Rat Pit), *The Honest Ulsterman*, *The Irish Times*, *The Irish Press* (New Irish Writing) and *Poetry Ireland Review* in which some of these poems were published.

The Gallery Press receives financial assistance from An Chomhairle Ealaíon / The Arts Council, Ireland.

Contents

THE RAINMAKERS

for my daughters

The Rainmakers

for Esther

We shake the young birches
hung with fat raindrops:
local showers that drench
only you and me; witch
doctors, I know, do it
better but this is
personal rainmaking,
private weather. Listen
to the laughter of myself
and my daughter under
the dripping birches.

Lough Eske Wood: The Blue Mist

Nothing much ever happens up here in
the stones and grass: a nondescript brambly
place full of saplings of hazel and ash,
you could pass it for most of the year with
barely a glance. Of course, if you really
fancied the place enough, you could sit there all day
in the sun and the rain and a ram-lamb
or ewe-lamb might dance you a jig on
the grass to the tune of a bird, or
a pheasant might crow, or the wind from the sea grow
lonely listening to the sound of its own
lonely voice. Nothing much ever happens
up here, as I say, until one day of
sun and shadows maybe, looking up through the trees,
you stand transfixed to see in the distance
a blue mist shimmering and floating in the breeze
as veil after veil of bluebells tremulously dare
to match the new shade of Spring a shower's
just washed into the May skies.

Print

I pause to rest on James's drystone wall
that's so low his meadow grass and flowers
crowd all over it when they're summer tall
and envy only the foxglove towers.

But something's happened since I sat here last –
I smelt the sweetness half a field away –
and what was yesterday grass and flowers
now, under the August sun, turns to hay.

And I know by the shape the windrows take
as sure as you'd know the print of a thumb
that James, for the first time ever, hasn't
taken a scythe to his meadow in Lacrum.

The Deaf Woman in the Glen

for Robert Bernen

In her own silence
in the silence
of the glen she is

a stone accepting
rain, a thorn bent
under the weight

of the wind, a heap
of bleached bones
in the gullet

of a dry burn. She has
hair whiter than
Scardan has in

winter; feldspar is
the pink grained
in the granite

of her cheeks; clouds
shadow the unplumbed
peat-brown

of her eyes and, perched
on this outcrop
of rock outside her

door and native
to her station as
the raven to its

crag, she is
locked in this
landscape's fierce

embrace as
the badger is whose
unappeasable jaws only

death unlocks from
the throat of rabbit
or rat and

moves, free yet
tethered, through
Time's inexorable weathers

in her solitary orbit
of the silent spaces
under the haunches

of her mountains and
the grey distended
udder of the sky.

A Snowy Good Friday

I take the snowy lakeside road today
past ice-frilled reeds that rustle in the sun
like cellophane; two stiff-necked whoopers eye
me from afar; the cold inflates a robin
on a white-capped stone and everywhere
the snow reveals the secret lives of men
and beasts: who would have thought, for instance, that
both fox and hare so much frequented this
bare place among the whins and rocks; that John
has twice already crossed this field today
with fodder from that haystack on his back
and stood, like me, under this overhang
to watch his steaming Friesians eat their fill
of hay that once was grass and flowers rooted
in the earth beneath their feet; who would have thought
that I was not the first to bowl pine cones
across the frozen shallows of the lake
and pit the drum-tight ice with fusillades
of stones like any vandal tempted by
a pane of glass?
                    The boles of trees and poles
and fencing posts are piped with ermine down
one side and sheep I thought last week were white
stand dazed and lost in dazzling drifts of light
as if bewildered by a landscape that
they thought they knew until it changed itself
into something as utterly strange and
new as that commonplace threadbare scrap
of daylight moon up there does night after night.
A wisp of wild geese in the distance fades
like wind-blown smoke; the woods are full of small
mysterious sounds as snow that fell as
silently as light now melts in tears
it sheds for Him whose death it mourned in white.

Blessings

Yesterday, for some reason I couldn't
understand, I suddenly felt starved of
trees and had to make tracks towards
the beeches of Lough Eske to set my heart
at ease and stand there slowly adjusting
myself to the overwhelming presence of all
those trees. It was like coming back among
people again after living for ages
alone and as I reached out and laid my
right hand in blessing on the trunk of
a beech that had the solidity but not
the coldness of stone I knew it for
the living thing it was under the palm
of my hand as surely as I know the living
sensuousness of flesh and bone and my
blessing was returned a hundredfold
before it was time for me to go home.

The Sinner and the Snow in the Glen

The first crocuses are
candle flames among
the starched altar-cloths
of late snow; the gate pier's

surpliced; under a
crucifix of weeping ice
nunneries of snow-
drops bow their heads,

pendulous and heavy as
thuribles; blood-red,
huge, the sanctuary
lamp hangs over Carn

on a faint chain of stars;
white inviolate aisles
creak under my feet
and the weight of my sins.

On Leahan

Another year has gone by since we heard the voices.
Innocence grows harder and harder to find and
death has taken its customary toll.
You have acquired your first grey hair.
Today as I climb the mountain in drifts of rain
the sea sends up its smoke-signals among the rocks,
the season for orchids has long since passed
and the ferns in the scree have begun to turn into
traceries of rusted wrought-iron filigree.
Points of mercurial light dance on the horizon.
I remember how on the summit that day
we heard the voices of playing children calling
out to one another in a language neither of us
had ever heard before and may never hear again.
We searched and searched but found no one:
not even the print of minuscule feet in
the soft black rain-pitted peat. Then the voices
faded away.

I have come here alone today to listen
once more but I have heard nothing except
the song of the wind in the rib-cage of a dead sheep,
the crying of curlews in the rain,
and now in the pub hours afterwards a man
tells me of someone who claims to have heard
the same voices we heard that day.
He speaks in a serious matter-of-fact way
like someone discussing the price of houses or cars.
I know I'll come back. Again and again. I might even
try to pick up some of the language.

A Roofless Cottage near the Horse Glen at Twilight

It was not my tears that watered the weeds in the hearth
and pocked the earthen floor;
only the clouds that grieve for the sun
weep for them any more.

It was not my hand that razed the chimney to the ground
and bushed the gap of the door;
only the wind that grieves for the void
laments them any more.

It is not my voice, nor the wind's or rain's, that you hear
in the room Neil pens his sheep;
only the voices of nameless doomed lovers
whispering endearments in their sleep.

The New Scholars

Their fathers tramped the length of the glen
to school. In sun sometimes but mostly in rain.
Their fathers tramped it barefoot, hungry.
They take the bus to a school in town.

Their fathers and *their* fathers learned to count,
to read and write: that was enough for them.
They had no eye for the light on high ground,
could see enough with the light in the glen.

But the new scholars, their wind-washed eyes on
the horizon beyond the lip of the glen,
stare up towards the sheep on high ground and
the light their fathers found too dazzling for them.

Undine and the Seal

for Anthony Glavin

He treads water to get
a better view of you:
the bald wet

dogshead gleams like
sunlit wrack: the eyes
are soulful

as my bitch's but
I know it is a bull –
the thick fat

neck of him; the bulge of
that brutal profile – rising
up to watch the wind

lick your body into shape:
cleft of bivalve, soft-
shelled limpets of

your breasts, the caves
Love will as surely fathom
as this seal

fathoms the cavernous
mysteries of the sea
again and again.

A Little Thing

She married late: an islandman who reeked
of fish and turfsmoke; the sea was on his
lips and in his kisses. She liked that and
in bed at night she liked listening to the way
the Gaelic suddenly came spurting out of
him the same time as his seed. A little
thing she missed: the trees of home, evenings of
splintered light, a net of shadows tangling
and untangling on the grass. He said that
she was mad, that others had tried and failed,
but she went on and now she has this stump
of hawthorn and a stunted sycamore
too low to ever tangle with the light.
Nothing will coax an inch more out of them.
She hates their sickly look. He laughs.
I told you so. A tree will never grow out here.
And kisses her to sweeten what he says.
She tastes the bitterness of salt.

In Memory of Patrick Boyle, 1905-1982

It was snowing in Glenveagh the day you
died, Moylenanav was white, and the red
deer watched us through fluted curtains of flowered
light; the torrents were writhing like serpents
in the heather and the waterfalls hung
out of the sky like the entrails of clouds;
the wind was skinning the boles of birches
and peeling the scabs of lichen from
the scalps of the stones and we were cold
that day as we ate our brown bread and cheese
under a dripping rhododendron but
not as cold as you were, Patrick Boyle, had
we known it then, laid out on your bed
on the far side of Ireland.
                              The deer turned their
beautiful buff-coloured rumps into
the wind and one stag with antlers twisting
out of its head like a thornbush out of
a split crag paused for a moment to stare
at us out of eyes as impenetrable
and mysterious as the wilderness
in which it was bred.
                        I remembered those
eyes when they told me, Patrick Boyle, that you
were dead and how you looked at me that last
time I saw you alive with the eyes of
a stag being hunted towards the ultimate
wilderness for which we are all bred.

A Soft Day

Myself and the dog. A thorn
that in autumn's all scarlet with haws now
shining with pendulous tear-shaped drops,
faint prints of wind on the pane of the lake,
the sea, crouched low in its lair on the
horizon, growling, baring its teeth, and,
far off on the side of a hill last night's
heavy rain has criss-crossed with the links of
a broken white chain, the wake of a hare
rising like smoke from long wet grass.
The applause of pigeons bursting out of the ash.

Wittgenstein

For years, deciding that he knew it all,
he switched to simpler, less demanding arts
until, discovering that he might be wrong,
he found that language determines how things are,
an element, not a precision tool,
something mind inhabits, a bird in air,
the fish of logic in a verbal pool,
and, boring some student from his wooden chair,
did he make him wonder if, alone in rooms
or silent for hours with Russell thinking
of sin and logic, there might not be *someone* who,
like Carmen or Betty, transcending
the limits of logic, reason, art,
could teach him the private language of the heart?

The Young Curate

He lived alone till she arrived and she
is one of them: a sheepman's widow
without child, soft and shapeless as a ewe
at shearing, her tongue barbed as one of
their fences. In the flagged kitchen at night
he hears their sing-song voices – English
uneasily riding the Gaelic undertow –
often the low growl of a dog.
He sees them sometimes silently filing
along the gravelled path towards
the kitchen door like sheep along
a mountain track. She feeds him well but leaves
him to himself: this is a world of men;
dogs and women come when summoned.
A sick call and she's up and out before
him to the hall and gossiping with
someone – as if death too could wait like
this man standing, cap in hand, inside
the door. In time he will grow used to
almost everything – the solitude, the
sparsity of trees, the reek of turfsmoke
from his clothes – everything except the way,
perfumed and fur-coated for the weekly
shopping trip to town, she settles
herself into the front seat of his car
like a clocking hen on a clutch of eggs.

Condy at Eighty

Going to sleep at night sometimes he
imagines he hears the cries of
young girls but wakes at dawn to

the bleating of sheep in the rain.
The wind has spared one sycamore but
each year sap still rises in it; in

summer it holds out the palms
of its hands to a miserly sun.
When he prays or swears the words

come in Irish: roots are the last
to die. If he had ever made love
the words would have come that way

too. The silence of the glen is
the silence at the bottom of
the sea; he has been drowning in it

for as long as he can remember:
a slow death. No one
understands his cries for help: it

is a private language he shares
with God and his dogs. The beds of
the torrents are paved with broken

stones from the heart of the mountain
and the light breaks loose from the clouds
like a wild thing; soon it is trapped

in shadows. In eight years these granite hills can break a working dog. It took longer to break him.

Revelation

I hardly knew him: I was only six.
And photographs don't tell you much: we put
masks on for them, learn certain facial tricks.
I caught his smell once in a mouldy suit

but how to disentangle truth from lies
is harder than evoking things by smell.
I can't forget what happened to her eyes
one Christmas night when she began to tell

me how they'd run away from home, and stopped.
It was enough: no need of anyone,
of snaps or odours then: this lean close-cropped
man was suddenly a hero to his son

and she a heroine, love's mystery
a torrent glimpsed from flat lands by the sea.

Going Under

Maybe the bishop thought he had the stuff
of sainthood in him. Like that holy man
whose rude stone hut still stands beside the pier.
He should have known better: bodies or souls
don't dry out here; he'd have gone mad without it.

Now, the island fast going under, listing
like a ship about to founder, each night,
terrified beyond reason, he lurched about

that tilting deliquescent deck until,
feeling the final convulsive shudders,
drunken lumps of it bowling him over,

he jumped and surfaced somewhere in Europe
with just a single island souvenir:
a listing ship trapped in a whiskey bottle.

The Writing Room

So much of his life was spent in this room
full of books, this mortuary for a heart
and mind embalmed, this sparsely-furnished tomb,
where, sounding the shallows and the depths, he charts

the wrecks of love silted up in marriage.
Nothing ever *happened* in this room.
What happened happened elsewhere in a rage
of love and hate: in the tiled kitchen's gloom

where the cat curled at the fire or a bee
trapped in a web indifferently eyed
another fire blaze as she and he
watched on TV how love was born and died.

Or in that red-carpeted upstairs room
where no one saw them shaping up to doom.

Letting Go

for Gerard Moriarty

He came today to take away her things
(I'm glad I wasn't there to see them go):
blouses and dresses, lingerie and rings,
even that tattered doll minus its toe.

I know we have to let them live their lives.
Not even love can change a thing like that.
Live and let live it was and it survived
the dramas of her love life and her hats.

But something deeper warns us to let go,
one of those things we never put in words.
Out of the darkness sunlit flowers grow,
under the silken cloak scabbards and swords.

Lives are for living: she must live her own.
The mystery of love is flesh and bone.

Blue

There's someone burning scrub down by the lake.
We smell the tang of it among the trees
and hear the crackle and the spit before
we glimpse blue smoke thinning in the breeze.

I wish I knew why things like woodsmoke
stir you so; I wish I knew the reason why
I am always losing you, as I lose
you suddenly now, to the blue of the sky

and the blue Bord Fáilte mountain in the lake
and all the blue translucencies of smoke
that dream such dreams of blueness in your eyes
you would not waken even if I spoke.

Death

We climbed all day through inundations and
inundations of light until
the islands shrank

in size to stepping stones across a burn.
Cloud shadows broke wild as March hares over
the screes; thick wet

lips of peat bared the stones of their teeth
at us; the wind combed partings white as bone
in your hair.

And then I saw the falcon fall from the sky:
arc after dark arc slicing the incandescent light;
I held my breath.

He nearly took you once: your grazed face
white as a tooth or a bone under
that fierce stoop.

The Island Cow

has the unhurried gait of
a barefooted woman balancing
a gourd of water

on her head. You know she
will never spill as much as
a single drop

of last night's dew from
her back nor tread on
a lark's nest

in the long grass. Her pace
is the pace of the tides,
full moons becalmed

in cloudless skies, scythes
in the stone-walled meadows.
Around the peg

of her tether through the field
of her gravity she moves at
the pace of the seasons.

The Hairs of her Head

for my brother, Michael

The nuns had cut her hair the day before
and now these outraged eyes in a white cropped
felon's head that scarcely dents the pillow bored
like gimlets into mine. *You* should have stopped

them doing this to me is what they said,
and said until she died – as if aware,
like Samson, of all the strength that
lay in the glory of her much-cherished hair

that was waist-long that childhood day she was
drowning in the Erne and black as her boots
as her sister grabbed and held on though she could see
strands of it snapping close to the roots.

All that's left of it now is upstairs, locked,
with her trinkets and things, in a box.

The Ashplant

For ages, buried in dusty bric-à-brac
and toys, it lay unnoticed in the lumber-
room until one night his tarmacadam
driveway rang with the thud of hooves and
heavy breathing sounds he hadn't heard for
thirty years. He ran outside and found this
bullock shying at its shadow on a wall
and four more lipping tulips on the lawn;
one roared and tossed its head in panic, sand-
wiched between the Escort and the Merc. He shooed
and semaphored, shouted and shook his pipe
at them, but they ignored this dervish in
his pin-stripe suit until suddenly he
thought of it and rushed inside and dug
it from its grave and, facing them across
a bed of trampled flowers and waving it,
he felt the magic come and watched them melt
back into the darkness where a barefoot boy
is standing near a wizened little man
in torn serge trousers and a knitted cap,
an ashplant like a sceptre in his hand
and at his back the kingdom of bog and rock
his son had flogged to German millionaires
before he was cold in Malin sand and stone.

Addict

Look, they say in the glen, is something wrong
that he's taking that old hill-road again,
I wonder what he thinks of all day long?

Look, the bogmen say, lost in the heather,
has he nothing better to do with his time
than take to the hills in *this* kind of weather?

Look, the forestry workers say, that's him
up there on that spink beyond the tree-line,
if he doesn't take care he'll break a limb.

Look, the sheepmen say, watching him throw
yet another stone on the summit cairn,
thon man's as light in the head as a sick ewe.

Look, they all say, look, will you tell me why
when he turns his head to the hills, there are
shadows like clouds in the blue of his eye?

Weathers

Slieve League's marbled with February snow
but larks are warming up here at its base.
Waves of unreal light break over sheep and cows.
The sea's white with acres of billowing lace.

The mountain inverts itself in the sky
in the lake, two different shades of blue.
A sea mist wears itself threadbare on stone.
Its lining of sky begins to show through.

You stride ahead into a cloud's shadow.
The dog's sniffing at some bones and feathers.
I follow. The way I have followed you
now for thirty years in all weathers.

John Clare

for Madge Herron

I am eye-level with harebells
and bees on a swelling curve of
the earth. The wind breathes on
the nape of my neck. I exchange
the integument of my body for
the pelt of the grass; beetles and
ladybirds inhabit the interstices
of my bones, explore the valves of
my heart. I insert my fingers
into the moist orifices of earth,
bruise my lips on clay and stones.
The swish of birds' wings brushes
against my ears like the silken
passage of girls in long dresses.
I enter the secret places where
worms turn the world on
their shoulders and pass the earth
through the alembic of their guts.
In the labyrinth of the green
forest I find them: a hare's foot,
horseshoes, a rainbow of lichen.
Someone calls me. The keeper comes,
trampling the light underfoot,
speaking a familiar language
I am trying to unlearn.
His words clash with the pealing
of birds, the tongued bells of flowers.

The Blue Boat

How do I know that the wrecked blue boat
asleep in the long grass under the alder
dreams it is whole again and still afloat?

Because when I passed it by one night last week
and the wind made a sudden stir in
the trees I heard the sound of timbers creak
and the swish of a keel in the lake.

from

IN THE LIGHT
ON THE STONES

Death of Thady

He could not tell you why
he loves the place so much – and
love's a word that he would never use.

He could not tell you why
there is no other place where
he walks taller than Errigal
and plants his feet like dolmens in
a wind-scoured land of scant grass and scanter sky.

He could not tell you why,
when he lay ailing in the warm bright ward,
the dark glens and the lonely
lakes in the sky and the flagged
cabin cold and bare as a prison-cell
were heaven to him as sure as this was hell.

He could not tell you why,
after the priest had gone
and the nurse indifferently watched him die,
he suddenly saw the hill-wind swirling
the turf-mould on the ward-room floor
and counted the last of his sheep filing
like mourners through the gap of the door.

An Oak in the Glen

He is ploughing
the lea field
with the brown mare
the way
his father and
his father's father
ploughed it;

he is taking
the burn hill
under a streamer of gulls
the way
his father and
his father's father
took it;

he is stooping
under a yoke
heavier than his mare's
the way
that stunted oak
stoops in the wind
from the sea;

the way
it was stooped
in the wind
from the sea
when his father
and his father's father
ploughed this lea;

the way
it will still be stooped
in the wind
from the sea
when his children and
his children's children
plough this lea.

Condy

He lives alone in the shadow of
mountains; his tilted stony acres
fray the clouds; he takes
eight years out of a dog and knows
his ewes better than the sons
he never had. The horizon is
his fence, his sheep range free
and yet his mind is
penned, his spirit tethered. He climbs
through darkness into
the light on summits but hears
no voices from a cloud. He fears
death – the rickle of bleached
bones in lonely places – and in drink
weeps for himself and his brothers
and for all the others
on whom the shadow of mountains
fell.

The Octogenarian in the Glen

Was it for this
he enriched her body with a spendthrift
abandon his lean acres craved in lime
yet broke her on a standing stone
as hard and inexorable as Time?

Was it for this
he shipped crop his loins had sown
on flesh and bone overseas like bags
of Banner seed and limed the land
too late for beasts no son of his would need?

Was it for this
he cast her, spent as a kelt, alongside
the corpse of her stillborn tenth child and
hardened his heart against the knife of a wind
sharper than March hones on the hills of Disert?

Was it for this
he tholed the gnawing teeth of the seasons
that stripped his spirit to the bone until
it was as cold as a granite boulder
the glacier once scoured out of Gaguin?

To stand alone
in his doorway at nightfall and watch, high above
dewfall and hawkfall, the sky seeded with stars
as barren as he wished in Christ's name his own
seed had been all the times
he'd opened her for another lost crop.

Fossil

They make a space for him who inhabits space
as a star inhabits the loneliness of it.
He stands on his own at the back of the thronged hall,
a long great-coat corded round the cairn of his body.
He steams in the heat and a pool of dampness gathers
about him and the sheepdog lying at his feet.
The peaked cap's a fungus growing out of his head,
the black rubber boots are bollards of eroded peat.
He lights up with hunched shoulders, huge hands cupped
round the bowl of the pipe, the sound of the wind that matts
wisps of the Grey Mare's Tail on the haunches of Suhill
whorled in his ears forever like the sea in a shell.
Smoke clouds the weathered granite of his face.
Suddenly the dog pricks up its ears, watching
his lips, waiting for a signal from him
to rout this pen of bleating sheep good
for neither dipping nor shearing.
But its master dreams, has a rapt faraway
look in his eyes as if already nostalgic for
the vast acreage of sky outside. He's calculating
the price he should get for his ewes at Brockagh Fair.

The Last Drover

For fifty years he travelled light into
every kind of darkness and saw more
winter dawns than was good for man or beast.

He wore the same serge suit summer
and winter indifferent as a whin bush to
the wind and rain that bent him in the end.

He slept on his feet like them listening
for the silences that woke him when
they softened through a gap or

bunched in sudden terror of a shadow.
He knew the stones of his roads better
than the corns on his feet.

Their heat warmed him on bitter nights.
They lowed to their own kind across stone walls and ditches.
He talked out loud to himself in the dark.

I mourn him now who left no deeds or songs
to set against the curlew's desolating cry at dawn,
who left no deeds or songs at all.

The Caul

for Pauline

You came up in the doctor's trawl that day:
you and your twin sister in the same net:
fish out of water, drowning in air, two
spring-run six-pound salmon, slippery, wet.

But *you* were born with a caul on your head,
a lucky charm against drowning at sea.
Before you touched the deck the doctor had
your birth-cap promised to Nahor the Quay.

Sometimes when we're sailing to the islands
and the half-decker lurches in a squall
I look at you and wish we'd kept that cap:
once is enough to come up in a trawl.

Elegy for the Islanders

They died elsewhere but their graves are here
and these bare gables are their headstones.

Their strong hearts faltered long before their
roof-beams fell and their hearthstones, cold

as their bones in an alien earth, mourn the memory
of their fires in diamonds of black.

I walk on the lichened stones of their graves
and a split flag cracks as their hearts cracked

once. I hear their death-rattles deep down
in the gullet of the sound and taste the salt

of their tears on the wind. Tears will wear out
a stone but what will a heart wear out but itself?

They wore out their hearts and left nothing here
but stones washed by the tides of their tears.